It's time for
COWS IN ACTION

Genius cow Professor McMoo and
his trusty sidekicks, Pat and Bo,
are star agents of the C.I.A.
– short for COWS IN ACTION!
They travel through time, fighting
evil bulls from the future and
keeping history on the right track ...

Find out more at
www.cowsinaction.com

Read all the adventures of McMoo, Pat and Bo:

www.cowsinaction.com

Also by Steve Cole:

ASTROSAURS

ASTROSAURS ACADEMY

www.astrosaurs.co.uk

The Moo-Lympic Games

Steve Cole

Illustrated by Woody Fox

RED FOX

THE MOO-LYMPIC GAMES
A RED FOX BOOK 978 1 862 30884 8

First published in Great Britain by Red Fox,
an imprint of Random House Children's Books
A Random House Group Company

This edition published 2010

1 3 5 7 9 10 8 6 4 2

Text copyright © Steve Cole, 2010
Cover illustration and cards © Andy Parker, 2010
Illustrations by Woody Fox, copyright © Random House Children's Books 2010

The right of Steve Cole to be identified as the author
of this work has been asserted in accordance with
the Copyright, Designs and Patents Act 1988.

The Random House Group Limited supports the Forest Stewardship
Council (FSC), the leading international forest certification organization.
All our titles that areprinted on Greenpeace-approved FSC-certified paper
carry the FSC logo. Our paper procurement policy can be found at
www.rbooks.co.uk/environment.

Mixed Sources
Product group from well-managed
forests and other controlled sources
www.fsc.org Cert no. TT-COC-2139
© 1996 Forest Stewardship Council
FSC

Set in 16/20pt Bembo Schoolbook

Red Fox Books are published by Random House Children's Books,
61–63 Uxbridge Road, London W5 5SA

www.**kids**at**randomhouse**.co.uk
www.**rbooks**.co.uk

Addresses for companies within The Random House Group Limited
can be found at: www.randomhouse.co.uk/offices.htm

THE RANDOM HOUSE GROUP
Limited Reg. No. 954009

A CIP catalogue record for this book is available
from the British Library.

Printed and bound in Great Britain by
CPI Bookmarque, Croydon CR0 4TD

For the one and only
Woody Fox

★ THE C.I.A. FILES ★

Cows from the present —
Fighting in the past to protect the future . . .

In the year 2550, after thousands of years of being eaten and milked, cows finally live as equals with humans in their own country of Luckyburger. But a group of evil war-loving bulls — the Fed-up Bull Institute — is not satisfied.

Using time machines and deadly ter-moo-nator agents, the F.B.I. is trying to change Earth's history. These bulls plan to enslave all humans and put savage cows in charge of the planet. Their actions threaten to plunge all cowkind into cruel and cowardly chaos . . .

The C.I.A. was set up to stop them.

However, the best agents come not from 2550 — but from the present. From a time in the early 21st century, when the first clever cows began to appear. A time when a brainy bull named Angus McMoo invented the first time machine, little realizing he would soon become the F.B.I.'s number one enemy . . .

COWS OF COURAGE —
TOP SECRET FILES

PROFESSOR ANGUS MCMOO

Security rating: Bravo Moo Zero

Stand-out features: Large white squares on coat, outstanding horns

Character: Scatterbrained, inventive, plucky and keen

Likes: Hot tea, history books, gadgets

Hates: Injustice, suffering, poor-quality tea bags

Ambition: To invent the electric sundial

LITTLE BO VINE

Security rating: For your cow pies only

Stand-out features: Luminous udder (colour varies)

Character: Tough, cheeky, ready-for-anything rebel

Likes: Fashion, chewing gum, self-defence classes

Hates: Bessie Barmer, the farmer's wife

Ambition: To run her own martial arts club for farmyard animals

PAT VINE

Security rating: Licence to fill (stomach with grass)

Stand-out features: Zigzags on coat

Character: Brave, loyal and practical

Likes: Solving problems, anything Professor McMoo does

Hates: Flies not easily swished by his tail

Ambition: To find a five-leaf clover — and to survive his dangerous missions!

Prof. McMoo's
TIMELINE OF NOTABLE
HISTORICAL EVENTS

4.6 billion years BC

PLANET EARTH FORMS

(good job too)

13.7 billion years BC

BIG BANG - UNIVERSE BEGINS

(and first tea atoms created)

23 million years BC

FIRST COWS APPEAR

(23 million is my lucky number!)

1700 BC

SHEN NUNG MAKES FIRST CUP OF TEA

(what a hero!)

7000 BC

FIRST CATTLE KEPT ON FARMS

(Not a great year for cows)

1901 AD

QUEEN VICTORIA DIES

(she was not a-moo-sed)

(by an Egyptian geezer)

2550 BC

GREAT PYRAMID BUILT AT GIZA

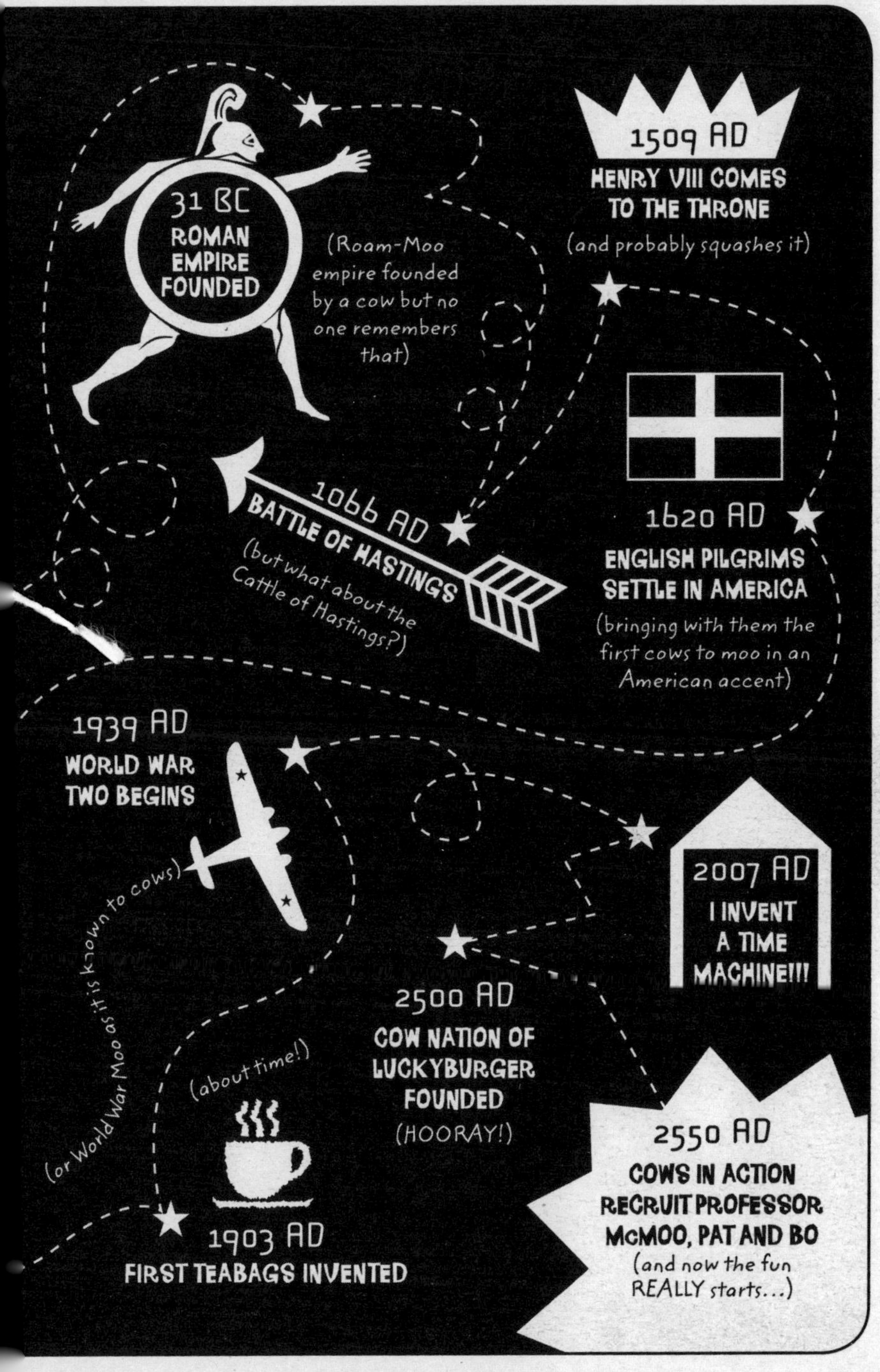
31 BC
ROMAN EMPIRE FOUNDED
(Roam-Moo empire founded by a cow but no one remembers that)
1509 AD
HENRY VIII COMES TO THE THRONE
(and probably squashes it)
1066 AD
BATTLE OF HASTINGS
(but what about the Cattle of Hastings?)
1620 AD
ENGLISH PILGRIMS SETTLE IN AMERICA
(bringing with them the first cows to moo in an American accent)
1939 AD
WORLD WAR TWO BEGINS
(or World War Moo as it is known to cows)
2007 AD
I INVENT A TIME MACHINE!!!
2500 AD
COW NATION OF LUCKYBURGER FOUNDED
(HOORAY!)
(about time!)
1903 AD
FIRST TEABAGS INVENTED
2550 AD
COWS IN ACTION RECRUIT PROFESSOR McMOO, PAT AND BO
(and now the fun REALLY starts...)

THE MOO-LYMPIC GAMES

Chapter One

TERROR TIMES TWO!

"Nothing ever happens here," Little Bo Vine grumbled. "I wish we didn't live on Farmer Barmer's farm – it's the most boring place ever!"

"Well, I think it's nice to have a rest between adventures," replied her young brother, Pat Vine. "We're normally up to our necks in danger."

"Better than being up to my udder in boredom," Bo retorted. "I haven't punched anyone in ages."

Pat frowned. "You punched me yesterday!"

3

"Yeah, but I didn't even knock you out," Bo complained. "I'm losing my touch!"

Pat sighed. He was a light-brown bullock and Bo was a rosy-red milk cow. They were different in so many ways, but were both Emmsy-Squares – a special breed of super-clever cattle. Both Pat and Bo were about a hundred times smarter, braver and tougher than your average cow, which was *part* of the reason they'd been recruited by an elite squad of time-travelling cattle from the far future, the C.I.A. – better known as the Cows In Action.

The other part of the reason was a certain Professor Angus McMoo ...

"Pat? Bo?" An imposing, reddy-brown bull burst out of a rickety shed in the next field. "Anything going on? I'm bored stiffer than a concrete ironing board!"

Pat smiled. "Not you too, Professor!"

Neither the professor nor his shed were entirely what they seemed. McMoo looked like an ordinary bull – apart from the glasses he wore – but he was in fact a genius inventor, an expert in history and a lover of fine teas. He had combined all his skills to turn an ordinary cow shed into a super-fantastic *Time* Shed, an incredible machine that could travel anywhere in the world to any point in time (with a built-in kettle and a stash of tea bags hidden under a haystack).

"Oi, Prof!" called Bo. "If you're feeling fed up, why don't you take us on a time-trip somewhere?"

"I'd love to," McMoo admitted, "but I promised Director Yak we'd be on twenty-four-hour alert to help the C.I.A.

with their latest time-crime investigation. Apparently the F.B.I. is up to something very big . . ."

Pat shivered. F.B.I. was short for Fed-up Bull Institute, and its evil time-travelling members were always plotting new ways to rewrite history so that cruel cattle ruled supreme. "Sounds like we should enjoy this break while we can."

"Enjoy it? No way!" Bo yawned and stretched. "I want to be a Cow In Action again – being a Cow In A Field is pants."

But even as Bo spoke, a large cloud of black smoke appeared from nowhere, just behind her. Pat stiffened and the hairs on his coat stood on end. He'd seen smoke clouds like that before. They signalled that an F.B.I. time machine was about to materialize – and with it, a deadly F.B.I. agent . . .

"Bo!" McMoo shouted as a towering

shadowy figure formed inside the sudden
smog.

Bo turned to find a sinister bull-like
creature striding towards her. It had
glowing steel horns and green eyes that
were alive with evil. Gleaming bronze
armour covered its white hide. In place

of hooves it had huge mechanical claws.
T–266 was emblazoned on its chest.

"A ter-moo-nator!" Bo gasped.

Pat gulped – ter-moo-nators were
the F.B.I.'s toughest, meanest agents.
T–266 tried to grab Bo but she dodged
aside just in time, hurling herself to the
ground. McMoo ran and rugby-tackled
the ter-moo-nator. As the two of them
struggled fiercely on the grass, Pat ran
up and joined in the fight.

"Save some for me!" Bo complained. She leaped into the air and opened fire with her wobbling udder, sending super-charged milk squirting all over the ter-moo-nator. McMoo broke off his attack, blinded by stray milk. Pat jumped clear too, spluttering – only to run into something hard and pointed and silvery.

It was *another* ter-moo-nator – also clad from horn to hoof in gleaming armour!

Before Pat could shout out, the robotic monster – this one was marked T-122 – snorted stinky gas into his face. At once, Pat's eyes blurred and his head began to spin.

"Target Pat Vine stunned," droned the gas-breathing ter-moo-nator.

"Pat!" McMoo struggled to his feet, wiping milk from his eyes. "Bo, there's another robo-bull – and it's got your brother!"

"Give him back!" said Bo fiercely, kicking the second ter-moo-nator's

chrome tail. At the same time, McMoo
lowered his horns and butted T-122 in
the chest. But the metal monster clubbed
McMoo over the head with both
powerful hooves, knocking him to the
ground. Bo was about to squirt the new
arrival with another mega-milk blast
when T-266 jabbed her with its horns
and sent a
powerful
blue spark
right
through
her. As Bo
crumpled
to the grass,
T 266
smiled.

"Target Bo Vine also stunned," it rasped.
"Retreat with victims."

"Retreat," T-122 agreed, slinging
Pat across its shoulder and pulling out
a silver platter – an F.B.I. portable

time machine. "Destination: ancient Greece ..."

His head pounding, McMoo struggled up. He was about to lunge at the two ter-moo-nators when he heard an angry holler from the farmer's cottage close by. "HEY! Leave my livestock alone! No one's allowed to attack the animals but me!"

The professor groaned. "Oh, no. Not the farmer's wife – not Bessie Barmer!" He stayed down on all fours as the fat, chimp-faced woman stormed up to the ter-moo-nators. Bessie hated all the farm animals and longed to turn them into pasties. *If I give away my secret intelligence now,* thought McMoo, *my cover will be blown – and who knows what she might do!*

"How dare you try to nick my stupid animals," Bessie snarled at the robo-bulls. "I don't know why you're in fancy dress, but if it's ancient *grease* you're after, I'll belt you with one of my old

11

frying pans! One
of my ancestors
was a great Greek
warrior, and I know
the moves too!"
As if to demonstrate,
she struck a fierce
fighting pose.

T-266 simply whumped her in the
stomach, and T-122 snorted more gas
in her face. Bessie gave a yelp, and
collapsed with an impact that knocked
McMoo to his knees. The ter-moo-
nators stepped onto their portable time
machines, and a cloud of black smoke
spread out around them.

"No!" shouted McMoo. He tried
to grab the ter-moo-nators but it was
too late. They were fading from view,
vanishing into the distant past – and
taking Pat and Bo with them!

Chapter Two

HOT ON THE TRAIL

"I don't believe it!" McMoo slapped a hoof to his head. "Pat and Bo, cow-napped before my very eyes." As Bessie Barmer started to come round, he turned and raced back to his shed. "I've got to rescue them . . ."

But as he charged inside, he glimpsed a dark figure standing in the middle of the shed. McMoo took up a fighting stance, ready for action. But the bull who faced him was not metallic. He was burly and black and hairy, with powerful horns, cool shades and a purple sash hanging across his body.

"Director Yak!" The professor breathed

a sigh of relief. "The C.I.A.'s finest. Where did you pop up from?"

"From the twenty-sixth century, of course," said Yak, waving a thick gold platter – his own portable time machine. "I came here to warn you, Professor – our agents suspect that the F.B.I. plan to kidnap Pat and Bo."

"They just did!" McMoo kicked aside a hay bale to reveal a big brass lever and yanked down on it hard. A rattling, creaking noise started up as the shed began its startling transformation. Instrument panels slid into sight. A horseshoe-shaped bank of controls rose from the muddy ground and a computer screen swung down from the rafters.

"I'm sorry I got here too late," said Yak. "We don't know what the F.B.I. are up to, but apparently it has something to do with the ancient Olympic Games."

McMoo nodded. "T-122 said he was off to ancient Greece. And if the F.B.I. want to change human history, then that's a good place to muck around. Ancient Greece has influenced and inspired human language, science, law, philosophy, architecture – all that stuff – for thousands of years." He curled his tail round the take-off lever. "Let's try to follow those ter-moo-nators' time-trails and see exactly where they lead . . ."

In a storm of purple light and a creaking of timbers, the Time Shed took off at top speed. Yak held onto a haystack as it spun them about like a funfair ride.

The professor twisted dials and jabbed at buttons as the engines roared even louder. "We're going a long way back, Yak. A long, long, *long* way back—"

Suddenly, the control panel blew up in McMoo's face. He and Yak were thrown into the far wall, sending tea bags and buckets scattering, as the Time Shed juddered to a smoking, steaming stop . . .

"Ouch," said Bo, waking up to darkness.

The ground underneath her felt hard and stony, and she could hear the rhythmic swoosh of the ocean in the distance.

"Pat? Where are you?" She frowned. "Where am *I*?"

At once, Bo heard a grinding noise, then the stamp of mechanical hooves. "You are on an island off the coast of ancient Greece," grated an electronic voice. "And you are a prisoner of the F.B.I."

Bright lights snapped on. Bo saw that she was sitting in the middle of a round, rocky arena. Ter-moo-nator T-122 had stepped through a sliding door in the cave wall – and just behind him came T-266, holding Pat in a painful hoof-lock.

"Bo," he gasped. "Are you OK?"

"I'm better than these robo-bulls will be if they hurt you!" Bo growled.

"The cow will fight to protect her

brother," noted T-122. "Just as our masters predicted."

Bo jumped up crossly. "I'll give your masters a hoof sandwich!" But then she hesitated as four human-shaped shop-window mannequins filed into the cavern. "Nice try, but you ter-moo-nators are still the biggest dummies here!"

Suddenly, the blank-faced mannequins strode towards her in a menacing fashion. "Fight them," ordered T-122. "If you do not defeat them, they will destroy you!"

As the dummies approached, Bo raised her hooves like a boxer getting ready to fight. "Don't mess with me," she warned them. "I've got a punch like a sock full of rocks!"

Pat watched anxiously as one of the dummies lashed out with a plastic fist. Bo ducked and kicked it into the mannequin standing behind it. Both

went down in a heap. A third dummy
jumped towards Bo but she landed a
fearsome double-hooved wallop on
its blank plastic face, which sent it
somersaulting away.

The fourth dummy took its turn next,
joined by the other three as they got back
to their feet.

"Careful, Bo!" Pat warned.

"I'll clobber the lot of them!" Bo

shouted. Sure enough, she spun round
and tail-whipped all four before
launching into a whirling tornado of
awesome moves. Finally, the mannequins
lay in pieces, and Bo glared at the
ter-moo-nators, panting for breath.
"Now let my brother go – or you'll get
the same medicine!"

"Excellent," said T-122. "We have need
of your skills."

Bo looked furious. "What do you
mean?"

"You have proven yourself better
than the training robots. Now you will
take their place." T-266 tightened his
grip on Pat's arm. "If you refuse to help
us in our training programme, Pat Vine
is history – ancient Greek history, to be
precise." And before the exhausted Bo
could react, the ter-moo-nators shoved
Pat back out through the door, and left
the arena. The door slid shut behind
them.

"Little bruv!" Bo shouted helplessly. But there was no reply.

"I don't believe it," groaned Professor McMoo. Covered in soot, he struggled to his hooves and assessed the damage. "We were so nearly there – zooming down a time tunnel towards the very spot the ter-moo-nators took Pat and Bo – when there was some kind of explosion . . ."

"The F.B.I. must have set a booby-trap to knock us off course," said Yak.

"Brings a whole new meaning to *time* bomb, doesn't it?" McMoo helped him up. "Lucky for us the emergency stop kicked in."

"It kicked me halfway across the room." Yak saw that his portable time machine had been bent and broken in the fall, and sighed. "Well, we're stuck here now. Exactly when and where have we arrived?"

"I'd say we've landed about seven

days *after* those two ter-moo-nators. Poor Pat and Bo will already have been their prisoners for a week!" McMoo sighed. "It's 440 BC. As for where we are, well, ancient Greece was made up of city-states, sort of like counties – and we're in one called Elis, the location of the old Olympic Games."

"Then the F.B.I. *is* plotting something around the Olympics," said Yak. "And with all systems down we can't send a message to C.I.A. HQ asking for back-up."

"The energy banks will recharge in a day or so." McMoo bustled over to the Time Shed's costume cupboard. "In the meantime we must disguise ourselves as locals and start tracking down Pat and Bo." He rooted out tunics, riding cloaks and a couple of wide-brimmed hats, thankful that the C.I.A. supplied him with all kinds of unlikely outfits. "Did you bring a ringblender, Director?"

"I brought *two,* just to be on the safe side!" said Yak huffily, holding up the shiny silver nose rings. "I'm Director of the C.I.A., not the tea boy!"

"Shame," said McMoo. "I do love an expertly made cuppa." Ringblenders were handy C.I.A. gadgets. To human eyes, any Clever Cow agent wearing one would look like an ordinary man or woman – so long as they wore the right clothes. Only other cattle could see through the disguise. McMoo put in his own ringblender and checked his human-style reflection. It showed a handsome, tanned but very worried man. "Come on, let's get going."

"Whoa there, Professor." Yak, looking uncomfortable in his Greek gear, shook his head. "We're on our own on this mission. You may be a whizz at history, but I'm not. So how about some quick Olympic info?"

"You're the director, Director." McMoo turned to the TV screen in the rafters. "Computer? Give us the ancient Olympics file."

++ Ancient Olympics. ++ Hugely popular sporting event/religious festival held every four years from 776 BC to 394 AD. ++ The Games were held at Olympia and dedicated to Zeus, king of the gods. ++ The ancient Greeks believed that many gods — such as Hera (Zeus's wife), Ares (god of war) and Artemis (goddess of hunting) — lived on top of a mountain called Mount Olympus. ++ The Games lasted five days and were ultra-important. ++ Even wars were put on hold so that athletes and spectators could reach Olympia safely. ++ Events included wrestling, running, boxing, horse racing and the pentathlon. ++ Up to 40,000 people came to see them! ++

"Imagine the queue for the toilets," said McMoo, waiting by the door. "Now, really, we've *got* to find Pat and Bo."

"Then what are you hanging around here for?" said Yak, breezing outside. "Let's shift!"

Chapter Three

FRIENDS, FOES AND FIENDS

The night was cool and starry as Professor McMoo yomped over the dark Greek hills beside Yak. He felt miserable without Pat and Bo, and was worried sick at the thought of them being F.B.I. prisoners for a whole week.

Suddenly, Yak grabbed him and dragged him down behind a large bush. "Watch it. Something's going on up ahead!"

"How can I watch it if I'm hiding down here?" McMoo peeped over the foliage. By the shining white moon he could see a rabble of human figures chuckling and cooing and looking at the ground. Knives and swords hung by their sides, shining in the moonlight.

"Bandits and cut-throats, by the look of them," said McMoo. "Still, they seem to be in a good mood." He stood up and addressed them, knowing that his ringblender would make him sound like an ancient Greek as well as look like one. "Hello! I don't suppose you've seen a cow and a bullock around here? Or a couple of metal bulls . . . ?"

The ragged group whirled round to face him, drawing their weapons. Then their leader stepped forward, a gap-toothed leer on his scarred face. "Who dares to sneak up on Andros and his fighting band?"

"Sorry – didn't know you were fighting," said McMoo.

"*Or* in a band," Yak added, standing up to join him.

"A soft metal band judging by those golden goblets on the ground over there," McMoo added. "Freshly pinched, are they? Very nice."

Andros glowered at him. "You followed us to try and take them back, did you?" He raised his dagger and lunged forward. "Well, take *this*!"

McMoo blocked the blade with one hoof and Yak butted the bandit on the bonce. Andros went down – but his rabble rushed to avenge him.

McMoo gulped. "Er, Yak? Ever fought ten cut-throats at once?"

"There's a first time for everything,"

said Yak gruffly. He
uprooted the bush
beside them and
hurled it at the
bandits.

As the first two took a leafy tumble,
Yak whipped off his C.I.A. sash from
beneath his tunic and cracked it like
a whip. One end twisted around an
attacker's ankle; the bandit fell, tripping
the man just behind him.

"I always wondered why the C.I.A.
makes you wear those things," said

McMoo, batting aside two more of the thieves.

"The sashes also unfold into blankets for all-night spying missions." Yak demonstrated with a deft flick of his hooves, tossing the fabric over the remaining robbers and jumping on top of them, squashing them into the ground.

"Um ... I don't suppose they stop heavily armed soldiers in their tracks too, do they?" McMoo pointed to where a dozen men were advancing over the hill,

each clad in bronze and leather armour, their fine swords drawn.

"Retreat, lads!" yelled Andros, struggling up in a daze and freeing his men from Yak's sash. "The army of Athens is upon us!"

As the battered bandits fled for their lives, McMoo and Yak braced themselves for another fight. But then a commanding voice rang out from the darkness. "HOLD!"

The C.I.A. agents held their breath as the soldiers hesitated, hands on their sword hilts.

"Use your eyes, men," the strident voice went on. "These travellers are well-dressed, not ragged bandits – and behold, they have recovered our priceless gold goblets. They must have fought like wild tigers!"

As a cloud drifted away from the moon, McMoo saw that the deep voice belonged to a tall, tanned bear of a man with a well-groomed beard and splendid purple robes. He wore a bronze helmet crowned with a plume of horsehair. "What are your names, strangers?"

The professor bowed. "My name's Angus, and this is, er, Yakkylees."

"Thanks for that," Yak muttered.

"Strange names," the tall man observed. "Well, Angus and Yakkylees, know now that you have made a friend of Pericles of Athens."

Yak looked blankly at McMoo. "Perry-klees?" he echoed.

"Oh, my word. Pericles!" McMoo grinned. "The great war general of Athens, most powerful of all the Greek city-states. A wise and honest man, if the history books are right – and a proper hero."

"I see my reputation goes before me," said Pericles, smiling as his men retrieved his gleaming goblets. "But had these bandit dogs stolen from me and lived to brag of it, that reputation might have faded – which would never do!" He laughed uproariously. "Tell me, my friends, are you travelling to watch the Olympic Games?"

Yak looked at the professor and nodded. "We plan to keep an eye on them. When do they begin?"

"Tomorrow," the great Greek said. "I was dining with my fellow leaders in a private hotel when I was robbed. You are welcome to stay there for the duration of the Games as my guests. Consider it my way of repaying you for recovering those goblets."

Yak leaned closer to McMoo. "If this man commands crack troops he could be a good person to have on our side against the F.B.I."

"And to help us find Pat and Bo," McMoo agreed. He bowed down low to Pericles. "We accept your most gracious offer, big fella. Please — take us to Olympia!"

★ ★ ★

34

For Pat, locked up in a small cell looking out onto a courtyard, time was crawling more slowly than a one-legged ladybird with a broken crutch. He'd been stuck here for seven days, watching the courtyard grow smellier and darker as T-122 filled it with cartloads of animal dung! The pongy pile had grown and grown, until now it blocked his view of almost all the moonlit sky. He felt fed up, stunk out and very, very lonely.

"Oh, Bo," Pat sighed. "How I wish you were here!"

From time to time as the week dragged by he'd heard his sister's voice carry distantly down the corridor. *"Don't whack him like that, whack him like this . . . Never use a hoof-chop when a tail-swipe will do . . . I said wipe the floor with his butt – put that toilet paper down!"*

"What on earth have the ter-moo-nators been making her do all this time?" he wondered.

Suddenly, he heard a scuffling in the tunnel outside – and then a voice: "Get off me, you overgrown tin of stewing steak!"

"Bo!" Pat jumped up as his sister appeared at the bars of his cell. She looked exhausted, and was covered in bumps and scratches. And just behind her stood the menacing figure of T-266.

"Enter the cell," warbled the robo-bull, unlocking the door and shoving her inside.

Pat gave Bo a gigantic hug. "Are you all right?"

"Much better now I've seen you." Bo hugged him back. "Tin-head has been making me train twenty oxen in 'how to fight humans'."

"That explains why they chose you to replace those training robots," Pat realized. "They knew you'd do a better job. You're the best cow fighter ever."

Bo looked worried. "After seven days'

intensive ox-training I've got some pretty stiff competition."

"Now we have no further use for you." T-266 slammed and locked the door. "You will be disposed of shortly." He lurched away with a satisfied electronic chuckle.

"I'm worried, Pat," Bo confided. "Those oxen are Clever Cattle brought here from the future. Now I've trained them up, they've been taken to somewhere called Olympia – and there's no saying *what* they'll do."

Pat sighed. "If only Professor McMoo were here!" He managed a smile. "But since he isn't, I reckon it's time we went looking for him – and escaped!"

Bo frowned. "How?"

Pat kicked away the old sack he'd been given as a blanket to reveal a large hole in the ground. "I had to do *something* while I was locked up all day," he said, "so I used my metal water dish to dig out a tunnel! I'm almost through to the courtyard outside. With just a few more days' work . . ."

"Say no more." Bo wriggled into the hole and started burrowing like a demented mole. Pat held his breath –

but soon the thick clay of the courtyard outside began to crack and split, and Bo forced her way out to freedom! Grinning with relief, Pat wriggled through the tunnel and joined her.

But then the sound of approaching footsteps echoed from the adjoining tunnel. One set was metal; the others sounded heavy and human.

"Someone's coming this way," said Pat.

"And there's no other way out of the courtyard," Bo realised." We might as well go straight back into the cell – we're trapped!"

Chapter Four

OLYMPIAN DANGER

"There's only one thing for it!" hissed Pat. "We'll hide in that mountain of doo-doo."

"*Ugh!*" Bo groaned. "We'd be crazy to hide there."

"Exactly," Pat replied. "So hopefully the F.B.I. won't dream of searching it!"

Holding their noses, the C.I.A. agents dived into the dung heap! Pat kept his mouth tightly shut as he

wormed his way through the muck and came out on the other side, hidden from view. He saw Bo emerge higher up the dung pile.

Then a huge, hairy woman came into sight, her bulk evident beneath her grubby grey smock and cloak, pushing a large cart stacked high with cowpats. Behind her marched T-122. Pat breathed a sigh of relief as the woman parked her cart over the hole he and Bo had left. But that same breath caught in his throat as he realized the woman looked horribly familiar . . .

"I don't believe it!" Pat hissed. "It's a dead ringer for Bessie Barmer!"

Bo groaned again with disgust. "We meet her rotten old ancestors whatever time we end up in!"

"You were told never to come here, Barmo of Elis," droned the ter-moo-nator. "You were meant to send the dung over by boat."

"And so I have," Barmo replied in a high, gruff voice. "But this is the last load, and I want that gold you promised me."

"Very well," rumbled T-122.

"It wasn't easy pinching all this dung from the local farmers, you know," Barmo went on proudly, "even for me, the best muck-raker around. They use it as fertilizer for their fields, you see . . ." She frowned at the huge, steaming heap. "Mind you, I don't know how you're going to shift this lot to Olympia overnight ready for the start of the Games – or why you like dressing up as a cow in armour. Still, since you're paying—"

"Be silent," T-122 commanded. He reached under his metal breastplate and produced some coins. "Go now, and be ready before sunrise to help us the moment you hear the signal."

"Yeah, yeah, just like you told me."

Barmo took the coins greedily. "Now, empty my cart and I'll be off."

With a ripple of mechanical muscles, T-122 lifted the cart and added its muck to the pile. But as he did so, he noticed the hole in the ground and turned sharply towards the empty cell.

Pat cringed. "Now we're for it."

"Warning!" the ter-moo-nator warbled, horns flashing red and blue. "C.I.A. agents have escaped."

Seconds later, the bronze armoured form of T-266 clanked into sight and took in the situation at a glance. "The prisoners cannot have got far. Search this island and the sea beyond."

Pat swallowed hard: T-122 was lumbering away with Barmo, but T-266 had stayed put, glaring around the courtyard.

"It won't take them long to realize this has to be where we're hiding," Pat muttered.

Bo nodded. "Looks like we're in deep doo-doo in more ways than one!"

But then T-266 pressed a button on his wrist and a creaking, clanking noise started up behind the high courtyard wall furthest from the cell.

"Sounds like some kind of machine," Bo said. Then she gasped as an enormous robotic claw came gliding into view on the end of a flexible steel arm. The claw dug its blades deep into the dung, picked up a big helping and carried it off back behind the wall.

Bo was wide-eyed with alarm. "What was *that*?"

"We know this dung is being transported to Olympia," Pat reasoned. "That claw must be loading it onto some kind of vehicle. Maybe *we* could get taken away with it!"

The claw reappeared, its jagged jaws open and empty again, ready for another load. Pat and Bo launched themselves onto the top of the dung pile, and clung together as the claw closed with a clang around them, squashing them with a ton of muck – but hiding them from T-266's sight. Pat's stomach lurched as the claw lifted them high into the air, then dumped them into a giant container.

"Ooof!" Bo gasped as they hit the plastic floor.

"At least we made it out of the courtyard," said Pat, grimacing as more cow-pies rained down on them. "Now all we have to do is keep climbing the dung as it piles in so we're right on top when the F.B.I. unloads it all in Olympia. Hopefully then we can escape."

"The professor had better be out there looking for us," said Bo. "Otherwise there'll be nowhere to escape to!"

Even as Bo spoke, McMoo and Yak were following their powerful new friend Pericles and his soldiers up a steep hillside.

As the procession neared the brow of the hill, McMoo made out the bulky shadow of a mountain. *Mount Kronos,* he thought, *the highest point in Olympia.* Ahead of him, a flickering light stood out brightly against the night sky – and the view from the top of the hill made him gasp out loud with delight.

The fields below were a seething mass of activity, lit by great bonfires. Tens of thousands of people from all over the Greek world had gathered for

the Olympics. An excited hubbub of
music, singing and shouting rose up like
the smoke past the silhouettes of grand
temples, stadiums and stables. Market
stalls sold food and wine and spices,
perfuming the air. Jugglers juggled and
pipers piped and drummers banged their
drums. All around the fringes of the fields
and lower slopes of the valley there were
people sleeping rough, waiting for all the
Olympic action to begin in the morning.

Pericles led the way down the hillside,
his bodyguards waving a special banner

that warned others of his importance so they would clear the way. "Well, here we are, my friends," the big man boomed. "But before I escort you to the hotel, I must go to the Temple of Zeus to ask the father of all the gods to favour Athens in tomorrow's events. Come!"

"You won't believe your eyes, Yak," McMoo murmured. "The statue of Zeus inside that temple is one of the Seven Wonders of the Ancient World. Incredible!"

"Never mind the statue, I'm looking

out for ter-moo-nators," Yak declared. "Incredi-*bull*!"

A stone wall marked the boundary of the Altis, the sacred area of Olympia where the temples stood. As they entered through an archway, McMoo saw a magnificent building, chock-full of pillars and shaped like a stone horseshoe. "That's the temple!" he cried – just as a distant whooshing, rumbling noise crept into the starry sky. It sounded as though a jet was approaching, high overhead.

But then McMoo was distracted by a commotion right in front of him. Twenty oxen came bursting out of the Temple of Zeus and ran in front of the fine marble steps. They were being chased by

angry priests in deep-red robes.

Yak frowned. "Where did those oxen spring from?"

"They came charging into the Temple of Zeus out of nowhere!" one priest yelled.

Suddenly, the oxen stopped running and turned on the priests, attacking them with hooves and horns.

"By great Father Zeus!" Pericles exclaimed. "Guards, assist those priests!"

Five of his men drew their swords and ran at the cattle. Two received a hoof on the conk for their efforts, while three more were tail-whipped and then whacked in the face by a big bull's butt.

"Come and see, everyone!" A big hairy woman in a grubby cloak was yelling from the Altis's archway. "THEY'VE GOT PERFORMING COWS!"

"She looks familiar . . ." McMoo frowned as curious crowds flooded into the sacred area, attracted by the woman's

raucous shouts. "She must be a Barmer."

Yak nodded.

"Bessie's nastier ancestors are favourite recruits of the F.B.I."

Then everyone gasped as some of the oxen leaped and turned somersaults to evade Pericles's soldiers. The others struck dramatic poses on the temple steps and started mooing at the tops of their lungs.

McMoo and Yak froze. Unknown to the humans, the oxen were chanting in Modern Cow language: "*Down with people! Cows make war, not milk!*"

"These oxen belong to the Fed-up Bull Institute," McMoo realized.

Yak nodded grimly. "The F.B.I. plan is kicking off!"

Chapter Five

A SLIP OF THE DUNG

McMoo and Yak could only stand and stare as huge crowds rushed into the walled area, many joining the Barmer-lookalike in calling for others to come and see these incredible cows for themselves.

"The oxen are only attacking those who attack them," Yak realized. "They could cause a lot more damage but they're choosing not to. It's almost as though they're showing off."

"But why?" McMoo wondered. "And why is Barmer trying her best to get everyone's attention . . ." Faintly, over the roar of the crowds and the moos of the chanting cows, he could still hear the rumble of engines. Then the noise was swamped by human voices as hundreds more people tried to squeeze into the temple.

McMoo's eyes widened behind his specs. "Yak – what if this is just a distraction? What if Barmer and the oxen are putting on this show because they don't want people to notice what's happening *outside* the sacred area?"

"We'd better check it out," said Yak.

Leaving Pericles yelling at the wayward oxen and urging on his hapless soldiers, McMoo and Yak forced their way out of the Altis through the crowd of people. When they finally emerged into the cool night and stood panting for breath, the whooshing of engines had died right down.

"Sounds like an F.B.I. jet-ship in hover-mode," said Yak.

"And look . . ." McMoo pointed to the one person marching away from the crowds converging on the Altis.

"Shift!" the big woman snarled at anyone in her path. "Make way – Barmo of Elis coming through!"

Yak set off in pursuit. "Come on, Professor!"

"With you all the way," McMoo assured him.

The two C.I.A. agents followed Barmo as she scurried out of the Games area and onto the wooded slopes of Mount Kronos beyond. The noise of jet engines was louder here, and up ahead an eerie glow shone through the leafy branches of the olive trees, far brighter than the first signs of daybreak that were showing in the night sky. Bravely, McMoo and Yak crept closer . . .

And found a humungous, futuristic plane with an enormous crate attached to its rear, hovering in the sky above them.

"Told you so," Yak whispered.

Suddenly, the jet-ship fired a laser at the trees just beside them, burning the foliage to nothing in a blinding blur of light.

"It's clearing a path to the Olympic village," McMoo realized.

The agents watched as Barmo waved her spade up at the ship. It rose a little higher – and then doors opened in the crate's bottom and it started raining cowpats in a ferocious brown downpour!

An almighty mountain of the stuff was soon created. Barmo ran around in the dung-storm like a Native American doing a rain dance. As the plops splatted down, she sculpted and shaped the sides of the towering heap with her shovel, making sure the sludgy pat-slide flowed towards the Olympic site.

"This must be what the F.B.I. don't want the locals to see," said McMoo as

Barmo ran off again. "But why?"

"Hang on . . ." Yak pointed. "Something's moving in there . . ."

McMoo's jaw dropped as two dark and slimy figures emerged, slipping and sliding, from the dung mountain. They looked familiar . . . "It can't be . . . can it?" He jumped out of hiding, his hopes and heart rate rising. "Pat? Bo?"

"Professor!" yelled Pat, beaming with delight.

Bo cheered at the top of her lungs. She raced past her brother and grabbed McMoo in a mucky hug.

"I'm so glad to see you," said McMoo. "Though, to be honest, I'm less happy to *smell* you!"

"I knew you'd find us," she said. Then she spotted Yak, mooed with delight and pounced on him. "Yakky-babes!"

"Hello, Agent Bo," said Yak, blushing.

Pat ran up to be part of the happy reunion. "Professor, we've been trapped on the F.B.I.'s island base for a week!"

"I'm sorry I couldn't get to you," said McMoo. "Nice trick, sneaking out with the dung."

"If only we'd escaped sooner," said Bo. "I was forced to teach a load of oxen how to fight."

"Sounds like the oxen we just saw kicking up a storm in the Temple of Zeus," Yak realized.

"But why would the F.B.I. start an

avalanche of steaming cow-pies?"
McMoo frowned as he noticed a large
insect on Pat's dirty shoulder. "Hey, is
that a dung beetle? Never seen one like
that before . . ." The beetle had a red spot
on its shiny black back.

"There are loads of them in that
dung," Bo told him. "Nasty little things!"
As she spoke, the F.B.I. ship finished
dropping its dirty load and dipped down
towards the smelly heap. Squinting into
the morning sunlight, McMoo wasn't
sure . . . was that a figure climbing out
of the cockpit of the flying machine and

scrambling into the vast dung heap?

Then he turned as Barmo's shrill cry carried through the ripe-smelling air – she was coming back. "This way, everyone! Follow the oxen – if you thought they were amazing, wait till you see this . . ."

Pat groaned. "That's Barmo's voice. She's working for the F.B.I.!"

"So we noticed," said Yak.

"Now she's leading people towards the dung heap," said McMoo. "We have to stop her—"

But it was too late. Barmo was rushing back, minus her mucky shovel, closely followed by the twenty agile oxen. Hot on their heels was a vast crowd, with Pericles himself and the temple priests at its head. Just as the human hordes arrived, the jet-ship fired a red ray at the moo-made mountain. The stinky dark brown sludge was set aglow with weird energy.

The priests wailed and fell to their
knees. "Only the gods could shine so
brightly!"

Superstitious murmurs of agreement
floated up from the crowd, while the
other leaders of Greece's city-states
pressed forward. "What use do the gods

have for a dung heap?" Pericles cried.
"Our senses are surely bewitched!"

McMoo frowned as he noticed that
Pat's dung beetle was glowing a fierce
red too. It jumped off and ran towards
its dung-heap home. Meanwhile the
terrified Greeks ran about in a flap as

the jet-ship zoomed away, its curious task apparently complete.

"First cows who walk like men, now a great light and the muck of many cattle," cried the priest. "It *must* be a message from the gods."

"It is MY message!" thundered a commanding voice from somewhere inside the mountain of cowpats, prompting gasps of awe and fear. "The gods of Mount Olympus have abandoned you. Now, behold the gods of Mount *Moo*-lympus!"

"Hide," hissed Yak. The professor and his friends joined him behind a smouldering bush as a huge vertical crack appeared in the giant dung pile and grew wider, as though an almighty pair of crusty curtains was opening. White-hot sparks shot out from within the steaming pile, and everyone watching took a step back as a giant figure in golden robes emerged on powerful hind legs. His face was hidden behind a metal mask. His eyes shone as red as the rising sun. His beard was like a cloud of cotton wool curling down to his ankles.

"You are fools, humans!" the figure cried. "For hundreds of years you have dedicated your Olympic Games to Father Zeus, when you should have been dedicating them to me – FARMER MOOS, king of the cow-gods!"

Chapter Six

THE GAMES BEGIN

"What trickery is this?" snarled Pericles.

"No trickery," boomed Farmer Moos. "I am here in the solid, mooing flesh, am I not? Hungry for war, thirsty for sport and wanting world domination for elevenses."

"You are a poor replacement for mighty Zeus, strange cow," Pericles persisted. "Zeus can smite us with thunderbolts from a single finger. What can you do?"

Farmer Moos pointed his hoof and a crackle of electricity shot out of it, blasting an olive tree to smithereens. The crowd gasped. Pericles's face fell.

"So that's how he cut his way out of the dung pile so impressively," Pat murmured.

"He is an F.B.I. agent who's well on his way to becoming a ter-moo-nator," Yak observed.

"You humans have grown too big for your boots," Farmer Moos announced. "It is time you were taught a lesson. Therefore these Olympic Games will be different – you shall not compete against each other, but against cows – most favoured beasts of the gods of Moo-lympus. Do you accept?"

Shocked mutterings went up from the humans, and the C.I.A.

agents shared worried looks.

Pericles looked around at his fellow leaders. "This strangeness can only be the work of our *true* gods trying to test us. Am I right?"

The men nodded grimly.

"Then we must accept the challenge of this foul impostor," Pericles went on.

"Send your best athletes against mine." Farmer Moos grinned nastily, his red eyes aglow. "They shall be crushed."

"Can't we whack him one right now, Professor?" hissed Bo.

"Not with twenty Bo-trained fighting oxen as his bodyguards," McMoo murmured.

But Farmer Moos had heard them. He turned, saw the C.I.A. agents hiding behind the bushes and stalked over to confront them.

"So," he said softly, eyeing Pat and Bo, "you managed to escape my ter-moo-nators. But it will do you no good."

"It'll do YOU a lot of bad," said Yak. "We're going to get the whole of the C.I.A. on to you."

"We can call them from the Time Shed," the professor agreed.

"Just try it," sneered Farmer Moos.

"Tell me," said Yak. "What does the F.B.I. hope to achieve by messing up the Olympics?"

"Victory," hissed the evil bull.

"Er, false god . . . ?" boomed Pericles. "If you are quite finished talking to the bushes, perhaps we can get these Games underway, yes?"

Farmer Moos turned and nodded. "My oxen are ready. And so am I."

The Greeks headed back towards the playing fields in anxious silence. Farmer Moos, Barmo and the oxen followed them without a backward glance.

"Funny," said McMoo. "He could have given us away to Pericles and the others."

"So why didn't he?" Bo wondered.

"Never mind that, troops, here's the plan," said Yak. "Professor, stick with Pericles – stay close to where the action is. I'll head back to the Time Shed and try to get a message to C.I.A. HQ about what's going down here."

McMoo nodded. "The systems should be up again by now. But you might meet more bandits on the way."

"I'll go along to protect him," said Bo, grinning.

Yak nodded reluctantly. "And I'll give Pat my spare ringblender and these human clothes so he can help you keep an eye on things here till we get back."

"In the meantime," said McMoo grimly, "let the Games commence!"

A strange atmosphere settled over Olympia as the flabbergasted officials made ready to begin the Games. The thousands of people who'd come to watch squeezed together on the grassy slopes, speaking in excited whispers. A strong whiff of cowpats filled the air.

Pericles had wasted no time in asking McMoo to take part in the Games – and Pat too, once the plucky bullock had demonstrated some nifty fighting moves.

"It's a shame your friend Yakkylees ran off, Angus," Pericles commented.

"I fear we need strong, fit men now as never before."

"Can we really take part in the ancient Olympics, Professor?" Pat hissed.

"Yak told us to stay where the action is," McMoo reminded him. "I have a hunch there will be plenty of it in this stadium . . ."

Now Pat and McMoo were waiting in a wooden hut with a bunch of sweaty human athletes and the enemy oxen. The first event would soon be underway – a running race, seven times up and down the stadium. While the other

athletes limbered up, McMoo and Pat watched Farmer Moos and Barmo as they sat in their own hastily built stand close to the track.

"I just don't get it," McMoo admitted. "That F.B.I. jet-ship could have used its lasers to wipe out everyone in Olympia. Why are they playing sports instead? And what was that red ray they fired at the dung mountain?"

"I don't know," said Pat. "Farmer Moos doesn't seem to care that we're summoning the C.I.A. either. He must feel very confident."

McMoo sighed. "That's what bothers me."

Suddenly, a fanfare sounded, and they turned to see a group of musicians blowing long, narrow trumpets. Nervously, McMoo and Pat followed the human athletes over to the stadium, while the surly oxen trailed along in their wake. McMoo saw that the running track was made of packed earth, with limestone slabs marking the start line. Then his nose twitched as he saw Farmer Moos say something to Barmo. The big woman smirked and walked away towards the sacred Altis, her trusty shovel gripped in her huge hand.

Wonder what she's up to? thought McMoo. He and Pat took their places between two lean, tanned runners, Paul of Argos and Milo of Croton.

Pericles, together with several other leaders, stood in a similar stand opposite Farmer Moos. "You race for the glory not only of your city-states, but of all Greece," he called to the athletes.

Then the trumpet blared again, announcing the start of the race. In a blur of bronzed skin and patterned hides, the athletes burst into action! The oxen charged away, but the humans were faster. McMoo worked his hind legs as hard as he could, building up a punishing

pace. He thundered along the track, drawing level with Paul. Pat was just behind him, steam shooting out of his nose. They reached the end of the track, swung round the marker and headed back again so they were facing the slow-moving oxen.

The crowd was cheering and stamping and clapping. The nation's leaders were punching the air. "This is a cinch!" cried Pericles.

"He's right," Pat panted as they reached the point they'd started from and set off on the third leg. "We're going to lap those oxen easily."

It was true. The oxen were trotting quite slowly, still on their first length. But just as the athletes prepared to overtake, the oxen went to the toilet right in their path!

"*Urgh!*" yelled Milo, skidding in a cowpat, crashing into two other contestants and knocking them to the ground. Paul of Argos slipped and landed flat on his back.

"Unfair!" A short, stocky man called Diagoras, ruler of the city-state of

Rhodes, raised his fist at the oxen. "Cheats!"

"Doing a poo in a race is not against the rules," said an Olympic official sadly.

Pat found himself surfing a cow-pie too, smashing into Professor McMoo's backside with both horns.

"Yeowww!" yelled McMoo as he was propelled clear over two more cowpats and onto the back of an ox, who mooed indignantly. "Talk about added value," the professor said. "I'm squeezing the long jump *and* bareback riding into a bog-standard running race! D'you think the judges will give me extra points?"

"No," snarled the ox he was riding, throwing him clear.

McMoo hit the ground hard – and moments later was trampled by the other ox racers, lost to view in a storm of dust . . .

Chapter Seven

THE OX FACTOR

"Professor!" Pat yelled, running into the dust cloud to help his friend to his feet.

"I'm OK," McMoo assured him weakly. "Don't stop to help me, *keep running!*"

Pat gritted his teeth and quickened his pace, ignoring the stitch in his side. With a sudden burst of speed he overtook three oxen but couldn't stop two others from taking first and second place. He just scraped into third position. The crowd's applause changed to boos and jeers as the oxen strutted around.

"I declare A. N. Ox to be the winner of the race," proclaimed the judge.

"A. N. Other-ox takes second place, with newcomer Pat Vine in third."

Pat helped McMoo up. "Oof," said the professor. "I'll be a Cow In *Traction* at this rate." He smiled at Pat. "You did well."

"But not well enough," said Pericles sadly.

Pat glared over at Farmer Moos, who was sitting alone, looking smug. "Just you wait till Yak and Bo get back with reinforcements," he muttered.

Diagoras of Rhodes heaved a sigh. "Let us go to the Altis and pray at the Temple of Zeus for better fortune in the next event."

"Good idea," said Pericles.

"I saw Barmo headed that way earlier," murmured McMoo. "Come on, Pat, we'd better tag along. Pericles and his pals might be the F.B.I.'s *real* targets . . ."

He and Pat trailed after the leaders as they headed for the temple, the sound of the crowd's disappointment ringing in their ears. But once they were inside the cool, shady building, it was the cries of Greece's leaders that deafened them.

"What's going on?" cried Pat as he and McMoo pushed forward.

"The statue of Zeus!" wailed Pericles. "It didn't look like that yesterday."

McMoo frowned. The mighty statue was as big as a bus, a magnificent gold and ivory creation. It *should* have shown Zeus as a wise and powerful old man dressed in solid-gold robes and seated on a throne of wood, gold and

ivory. But now it sprouted enormous handlebar horns and its head was that of a scowling bull with a gigantic beard.

A bald priest popped up from behind the altar with a big smile on his face. "Welcome," he said, "to the Temple of Farmer Moos!"

"How dare you!" stormed Pericles. "This is *Zeus's* temple, not Moos's!"

The priest looked baffled. "Zeus . . . ? That name rings a bell. But, er . . . who is Zeus again?"

"The priest is bewitched!" Diagoras declared, and the other leaders nodded gravely. "Curse Farmer Moos. We should join together and crush him!"

"Those terrible sparks from his hoof would kill us all," said Pericles. "And what would our people do without us to guide them? No, if we are to defeat this impostor, we must show him that we are greater than his enchanted cows. We must win the Olympic Games."

"Well said," McMoo murmured. Then he thought he heard something in the temple – a creepy, scuttling sound. He looked all around the statue, but saw nothing.

"Look, Professor." Pat pointed at the priest's shiny pink pate. "He's got a lump on his head. He's been clobbered!"

"By something heavy and flat . . . like a spade," McMoo observed. "I bet Barmo conked the priest and then did a little dung-sculpting to make the statue look like Farmer Moos."

"This is truly a terrible day." Pericles looked at McMoo and Pat. "McMoo, you fought hard enough before to drive off a pack of bandits. You and your young friend simply *must* triumph over the oxen in the next event – the wrestling."

"Oh. Lovely." McMoo turned to Pat and lowered his voice. "The ancient Greek version's a bit tougher than WWF.

Anything goes – no matter how mean or brutal."

Pat gulped. "And thanks to Bo, those oxen are super-ultra-mega-tough!"

McMoo nodded. "Let's hope that the C.I.A. is on its way in force to take care of the whole lot of them!"

But the professor's hope was in vain. At that exact moment, Bo was out in the wild, deserted hills, tapping her hoof impatiently while Yak looked carefully around for landmarks.

"Come on, Yakkeroony," she grumbled.

"It was dark when the prof and I went out looking for you," Yak told her. "These hills

look different in daylight . . . But I think the shed's in this direction."

He hurried away and Bo trotted along behind him. Sure enough, just over the next rise they saw a familiar ramshackle box of wood and corrugated iron standing on a rocky slope.

"The Time Shed!" Bo beamed. "Hey – you left the door open."

"Let's hope we get inside before *they* do." Yak pointed up at the sky. "Here comes the F.B.I.!"

With a shudder, Bo saw the gleaming, boxy shape of the jet-ship fast approaching from out of the blue. Laser bolts sparked from its cannons! The light-blasts tore huge chunks out of the hillside close by, throwing Yak and Bo to the ground. They looked up and saw Ter-moo-nators T-266 and T-122 waving at them through the ship's windscreen.

"Shelter in the shed!" Bo shouted over the ear-splitting explosions. "It's our only chance!"

They zigzagged over the grass as the jet-ship turned and opened fire again. Another explosion went off right in front of them. Yak dodged most of the debris, but Bo was hit on the head by a lump of rock and fell to the ground. Yak ran back to try and help her up. "Come on, Bo," he said. "We're so nearly there . . ."

But then, as the jet-ship came to hover over the shed, he saw a door open in its side. The silver figure of T-122 threw out a rope and slid down it with breathtaking speed, landing heavily on the Time Shed's roof. He fired an electric blast from his horns, dropping Yak where he stood.

"This time vessel is now the property of the F.B.I.," the ter-moo-nator snarled. "And so are both of YOU!"

Chapter Eight

WRESTLING WITH DISASTER

McMoo and Pat were back in the athletes' enclosure. For the wrestling they had been joined by some truly towering men who looked as though they could bend steel bars with their big toes. But could they fight oxen from the far future, trained by an ultra-feisty cow?

Warily, McMoo watched the oxen as they worked out in the corner, skipping, doing push-ups or jogging on the spot. Then the familiar fanfare of trumpets started up.

Pat gulped. "The wrestling contest is starting!"

As the athletes entered the stadium, the excited crowds jumped up and down, cheering. The judges met each ox and partnered him with a human athlete before directing both to a different area. McMoo was paired off with the biggest ox of all, while Pat found himself up against a scowling young animal.

An expectant hush fell over the stadium. Pat's nose twitched. He glanced over to where Farmer Moos sat smugly, and frowned: Barmo of Elis was spreading dung all around the stand. What was she up to? Pat heard the chittering of the dung beetles and caught red glimmers in amongst the muck . . .

Then the trumpets sounded again, and an ox hoof cracked into Pat's skull. He yelped and fell backwards, rolling over and jumping to his feet again. The ox followed this up with a double-hooved punch – one of Little Bo's classic moves – but Pat managed to duck just in time.

McMoo's ox opponent tried to biff him in the belly – but the professor had expected that as an opening move: it was one of Bo's favourites! He jumped back, narrowly avoiding a savage ox-tail swipe, and lashed out with a right-hoof chop. But the big ox was too fast: he ducked under the blow and grabbed McMoo, lifting him up into the air – and dumping him headfirst onto the ground.

"Professor!" cried Pat in alarm, dodging a sneaky stomp-kick he'd guessed was coming.

Looking around, he realized that the human athletes were far less well prepared. The onlookers gasped and groaned as men were beaten like old reed mats, swung about like dirty washing and scraped over the dirt like living mops.

"No more!" squealed one muscleman as his opponent sat on him. Another Greek wailed as an ox smacked his bottom so hard that one cheek nearly fell off!

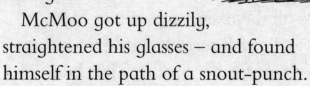

McMoo got up dizzily, straightened his glasses – and found himself in the path of a snout-punch.

He blocked the blow with one hoof and delivered an uppercut to the ox's chin. "Sorry, mush, but you were asking for it."

"Professor!" Pat cried, delighted by McMoo's recovery.

Unfortunately, still a little dazed, McMoo thought Pat was calling for help. He turned to check his friend was OK – and his enemy floored him with a big belly-slap. "OW!"

PARRRP! The trumpets sounded. At the end of the contest, only Pat and one of the Greek athletes remained standing, while all the oxen were still on their hooves. Pat felt terrible. Little Bo, acting out of fear for her brother's life, had trained the cattle only too well.

"I declare the oxen to be the clear winners by eighteen to two," said the judge solemnly.

Pat and the professor looked at each other helplessly. Farmer Moos laughed as Pericles and his fellow leaders fell sobbing to the floor. But the biggest shock came when the audience started to clap. The applause was ragged at first, but soon grew stronger.

"Well fought, oxen!" someone bellowed.

"Of course they fought well," yelled another. "They are cows, descended from Farmer Moos and all the gods!"

Pat stared at McMoo. "It sounds like some of them are actually starting to believe in Moos!"

McMoo frowned. "But how can they?" He watched as the oxen swaggered off to celebrate with Farmer Moos and Barmo while their vanquished human opponents limped back to the enclosure. "Come on, let's ask Pericles about the next event. Whatever it is, we've *got* to win it . . ."

Farmer Moos watched them head towards the despairing leaders. "That boy Pat is too good an athlete to be allowed to play on," he told Barmo. "Any victory for the Greeks slows down the success of our secret strategy. So" – he produced a dung beetle from within his robes and smiled – "this is what I want you to do . . ."

Miles away across the hills, Yak and Bo sat helpless and miserable on the floor of the Time Shed. T-266 was pointing a gun at them while T-122 inspected the controls.

"Now we know why Farmer Moos wasn't bothered about us going to call the C.I.A.," the director grumbled. "He'd already sent ter-moo-nators to the shed to head us off."

Bo nodded. She kept thinking she heard little scuffling sounds from behind the hay bales. *More of those horrible dung beetles, I guess.*

T-122 flicked a switch, and a loud raspberry blew from somewhere in the horseshoe-shaped console.

"What is the delay?" asked T-266. "Our masters have ordered us to take this machine to our HQ."

"Masters, eh?" Yak's ears pricked up. "So there are other F.B.I. agents here as well as Farmer Moos?"

"That does not concern you," droned T-266.

"Our time-trap caused a systems crash," said T-122. "The shed's drive systems are not yet back online."

"Unlucky!" Bo jeered. "Guess we're not going anywhere."

"Incorrect." T-266 looked at his fellow ter-moo-nator. "I will lower the tow-rope from the jet-ship, and you will secure it to this vessel."

"I don't believe it," groaned Yak. "They're going to *tow* the Time Shed back to their base — and us with it!"

Back in Olympia, McMoo and Pat — feeling very stiff and sore — had followed Pericles and the other leaders back to the Temple of Zeus. "After that wrestling match disaster," said Pat, "they're probably praying like never before."

But inside, the two agents found the smell of cowpats stronger than ever, and

the humans
standing
around in some
confusion. The
statue of Farmer
Moos was still
there, but now
all the paintings,
mosaics and
carvings of Zeus
had also been
given horns and
red eyes as well as long beards.

Pericles was scowling at the priest. "I thought we told you to change this statue back."

"Change it back?" The priest looked baffled. "But surely it has always looked this way."

"Er, has it?" Diagoras scratched his head. "Surely, it used to look like . . . like . . ."

"Like *Zeus*," McMoo called over.

"You know – big old man, king of the gods, lord of the sky."

"That's him, Angus," Pericles agreed. "Zeus, of course. This Farmer Moos is an impostor."

"How dare you!" the priest protested. "Moos is our great master!"

"*Zeus* is our master," said Pericles crossly. "You are unwell, priest. Lie down somewhere until you feel better." He shook his head as the priest scurried away. "I wish *I* felt better. My head throbs as though the gods were banging a drum in it."

"Mine too." McMoo rubbed his sore head ruefully. "I'm sorry we didn't get a better result in the wrestling."

"It's only to be expected," said Diagoras. "How can

96

humans expect to beat the glorious beasts of the gods?"

Pat frowned. "They're not the beasts of the gods, they're just very well-trained cows."

Suddenly, one of the Games organizers came in. "Gentlemen, please be seated in the stadium," he said grandly. "We are about to begin the pole-vault event."

"Splendid," said Diagoras. "My favourite."

"What are you on about?" McMoo protested. "The pole vault was never part of the ancient Olympics! It won't even be invented until 1850."

"You're mistaken, Angus." Pericles tapped his head as though a bug was trapped inside it, his eyes looked strangely glazed. "The pole vault is marvellous fun."

McMoo scowled. "What?"

The official gave him a withering look. "If you're planning to take part, sir, you'd better return to the athletes' enclosure."

As Pericles and the leaders wandered back to their stand, McMoo frowned at Pat. "Something's very wrong here – and getting wronger. Whatever the F.B.I. is planning, we're running out of time to stop it!"

Chapter Nine

PAT ATTACK

"Tell you what, Professor," said Pat. "While the priest takes a nap, why don't you put Zeus's temple back to normal? I can take part in the pole vault. I'll be pretty good – Bo and I used to vault over the farm gates when we were little, so I've had some practice."

"You can bet the oxen have had some too – unlike me." McMoo sighed, but then smiled at Pat. "At least someone on the human side will know what they're doing. Just be careful!"

"You too," said Pat, running off. "See you later!"

Alone in the temple, McMoo inspected

the statue more closely. It stank of
cowpats. He realized Barmo had used
ox poo to redecorate the statue. As he
broke off one of the huge, smelly horns,
a darkly glowing dung beetle scuttled
out from inside and sat on his hoof.

"Another one of those weird insects,"
he murmured, feeling slightly dizzy.

"Well, I'm sure Barmo put you here for a good reason. She is a servant of the great Farmer Moos after all . . ." He gasped, shook his aching head to clear it. "What am I saying? Moos is an F.B.I. agent. Moos is the enemy!" The professor suddenly dropped the beetle – which scuttled straight back towards the horn stump – and staggered away. He found more cow dung piled in the cool shadows of the temple, and another glowing dung beetle to go with it.

Then he remembered how the stadium stank of dung too. "Maybe Barmo hasn't just been shovelling up ox dung around here. Maybe she's been laying it *down* instead – so the beetles can spread!"

Hurrying out to check the grassy slopes of the stadium for cowpats, McMoo saw that the pole-vaulting contest was already underway. The bar was a piece of bamboo, laid across two long spears sticking vertically out of the ground.

An ox
ran
up to
a small
pit in
the track,
planted a
long stick in its centre and
propelled himself up and
over the bamboo bar before
landing neatly on all fours. The
spectators jumped up to clap and
cheer, more loudly than before.

And as they did so, McMoo saw
that cowpats had been scattered all
over the stadium! "Just as I thought,"
he muttered. Some of the people had
even been sitting in the stuff. From the
conversations he heard and the noisy
cheers, the spectators simply wanted to
see the oxen beating the humans. And
here and there he saw more beetles
quietly glowing . . .

"Of course . . ." McMoo breathed. "*That's* what the F.B.I.'s up to!"

As another ox hurtled over the high bar, the professor ran off to the stand where Farmer Moos sat watching the Games.

"I know what you're doing!" McMoo declared.

"Oh?" Farmer Moos looked at him. "Well, I hope you know what *you* are doing – daring to come here alone."

"Just keeping you company while Barmo's out spreading more muck and menace," said McMoo, ignoring the threat. "It's those glowing dung beetles, isn't it? They're messing with people's minds. When your jet-ship fired that red ray at Mount Moo lympus, it activated them somehow. And now they're changing how the humans think. They're starting to accept *you* as the ruler of their gods!"

"And so they should," said Farmer Moos, clapping as another ox somersaulted over the bar.

"That's why Barmo made the images of Zeus look more like you," McMoo went on. "To back up what the beetles are telling people to believe."

Farmer Moos smiled. "You're very clever."

McMoo shook his head. "Not clever enough to work out why you're making the ancient Greeks go pole-vaulting."

"A simple test to see how easily they can be influenced," Farmer Moos admitted. "You see, the more downhearted and distracted they are, the more vulnerable their minds become to our brainwashing."

"So each Olympic failure for the

humans has made the beetles' work easier," McMoo realized.

Farmer Moos tutted as Milo the athlete raced up to the bar and smashed straight through it — to jeers and boos from the baying audience. "Both organizers and spectators now see the pole vault as quite normal, when in fact they have never heard of it before — a sure sign that they will soon accept me as their absolute ruler without question. They will believe it has always been so."

"And that's why you didn't blow anyone up with your jet-ship's lasers or hurt them with your electric hoof," stormed McMoo. "You've got the leaders of every city-state in ancient Greece sitting over there. And by the time your *Moo*-lympic Games are over they'll be swearing blind that Zeus is Moos and cows are the animals of the gods. They'll go home telling their people that cows are to be *served* by humans. Am I close?"

"Close enough," the F.B.I. agent agreed quietly. "The humans will be completely brainwashed, and evil warlike cows will be their masters."

"Oh, yeah? Well, I bet your brainwashing can still be reversed," said McMoo. "And that's just what I plan to do!"

Farmer Moos shook his head. "Not if you value the life of Pat Vine."

"Pat?" McMoo turned back to the events in the stadium and saw Pat running with the pole, just about to vault. The pole hit the pit, Pat sailed through the air . . .

And something else sailed through the air too.

A fresh cow-pie!

It flew out from the crowd and hit the ground in the very spot where Pat was due to land. Pat desperately tried to twist round and avoid it – but the pole snapped and he struck the muck face

first with a squelching *thump*.

"Pat!" McMoo turned to the judges: "Oi, ref! Foul!"

"*Very* foul," Pat groaned.

"Throwing cowpats isn't against the rules," said the judge calmly.

"Pat, over here!" McMoo yelled, but he could barely be heard over the crowd's laughter at Pat's predicament. "Get that stuff off you, quick . . ."

But a dung beetle had already burst out of the sludgy mess and quickly jumped down Pat's tunic without him noticing.

"The beetles are only effective on

cattle at close range," Farmer Moos explained. "Your genius mind can resist, no doubt – but I wonder how Pat will fare?"

"He'll be fine," McMoo promised, "because I'll knock that thing off him."

But as Pat ran over, Farmer Moos called out, "This person is your enemy, Pat."

"Don't be ridiculous," McMoo spluttered.

"You . . ." Pat looked at McMoo strangely – the same look the priest in the temple had given Pericles. "You are . . . my enemy." He lowered his horns threateningly.

"Oh, Pat, *no*!" The professor rounded on Farmer Moos. "You'll never win. Bo and Yak will soon have the whole C.I.A. on to you!"

But the F.B.I. agent burst into sinister mechanical laughter as, with a roar of engines, the jet-ship sailed across the sky

– with a large, ramshackle building dangling from a rope beneath it. "The Time Shed? Hey!" McMoo shook his hoof at the vanishing vessels. "Come back!"

"You see, Professor?" said Farmer Moos smugly. "Bo and Yak have been captured by my ter-moo-nators. Your time machine has been confiscated. Pat Vine now serves the F.B.I. And soon, the greatest civilization of the ancient world will serve us without question." His voice rose in pitch and volume. "Admit it, Professor – this time the F.B.I. has won, and there is nothing you can do about it!"

Chapter Ten

THE MOO-LYMPIANS

"There's always *something* I can do,"
McMoo told Farmer Moos. "I can
RUN!" With a last helpless look at the
brainwashed Pat, he turned and sprinted
off.

"There's nowhere to run to, Professor!"
Farmer Moos yelled after him.

"Maybe not," muttered McMoo.
"But there might just be somewhere
to *sail* to . . ." He hared round the back
of the stadium and saw Barmo of Elis
emerging from the crowd with her spade.
"*Oi!* You!"

"Uh-oh." Barmo started to run,
but McMoo soon caught up with her,

snatched her shovel away and sat her down on the grass.

"I knew it was you who slung that pat at Pat," he panted. "Well, now *you're* in the poo!"

"I will answer none of your questions," said Barmo, a strange look in her eye. "I serve only Farmer Moos and the cows of the sky."

"I suppose you served them of your own free will at first," said McMoo sadly. "But now you've been beetle-brainwashed like everyone else." Then suddenly, he brightened as an idea struck him. He plucked out his ringblender and shrugged off his clothes, so his human appearance vanished. Then he put his ringblender back in, so the women could still understand him.

"See me now, Barmo? I'm a bull of the gods myself, and I need to get back to my time machine. How can I reach Farmer Moos's base?"

"I have a boat," said Barmo. "I have rowed to the gods' island with the gift of dung. I can take you there too, my lord."

"Good! We'll leave at once," ordered McMoo. "I've got friends to rescue – and a world to save!"

Swinging high above the ground, Bo was feeling airsick. She was holding onto the doors for support as T-266 headed for the F.B.I. base, dangling  McMoo's tumbledown shed from the end of the tow-rope.

"I'm used to *my* existence hanging by a thread," she murmured, "but it's a first for the Time Shed!"

T-122 said nothing, metal face impassive as he studied the horseshoe-shaped bank of controls.

Bo looked across at Yak. He was leaning over a haystack with his back to Bo and the ter–moo–nator, and seemed to be muttering to himself. "Hey – are you feeling all right?" she wondered.

Yak slowly straightened, turned to Bo and winked. "Right now, I feel better than I have for ages."

T-122 glared at him. "That will change when you are given to the Moo-lympians."

Yak frowned. "Are they your mysterious masters?"

"Yes," said T-122 simply.

"I guess we don't have much time left." Yak crossed to Bo and lowered his voice. "If we're going to turn the tables on that ter–moo–nator, we must act soon!"

★　★　★

113

An hour later, McMoo was approaching
the same island by boat. With Barmo
lending her impressive weight to the oars,
they hurtled over the water. The professor
felt a shiver as the F.B.I. base came into
sight.

When they drew closer, he saw a
wooden jetty standing beside a door
in the rock – which was clearly their
destination. "Perhaps I'd better swim
from here," mused McMoo.

"Don't bother," came a grating voice
as the door in the rock slid open. "You're

in deep enough water already."

"Ah . . ." The professor sighed as T-266 strode out, carrying a gun. "Well, saves me having to sneak inside anyway. How are my friends Yak and Bo?"

"They are in the courtyard with your time vessel," droned the ter-moo-nator, the sun gleaming off his bronze armour. "The Moo-lympians will decide their fate."

With Barmo blocking any escape just by walking behind him, McMoo followed the robo-bull through stone tunnels until they reached a whiffy, muck-stained courtyard. There was the Time Shed, still tied up with steel ropes, some of which trailed over a high wall at the rear of the yard. And there, on the ground, leaning weakly against T-122 was . . .

"Yak!" McMoo beamed at him. "Good to see you, big fella."

"*Bad* to see you've been captured too," Yak replied.

The professor shrugged. "Where is Bo?"

"Bo's not feeling herself," said Yak. "She's flat out in the shed. We tried to overpower metal-pants here before we landed – but it didn't work out."

McMoo scowled at T-122. The ter-moo-nator's metal helmet was askew and its chest-plate full of dents. "Glad to see the pair of you got some blows in first, anyway."

"How about Pat?" asked Yak. "Is he OK?"

"Not really," McMoo admitted, and was surprised to see T-122 stiffen.

"Pat Vine has fallen victim to our brain-beetles," droned T-266. "Incredible insects with telepathic powers."

McMoo nodded. "I knew it! They talk with their minds."

"The beetles were bred in F.B.I. labs with one purpose – to weaken the will of human beings," T-266 went on. "Soon we shall shine our 'switch-off' ray on the beetles, and their minds will stop transmitting the brainwashing signal – leaving a single overriding thought in the humans' heads."

"That they worship cows," McMoo realized grimly. "That they have *always* worshipped cows."

"We shall build many mind-altering heaps like Mount Moo-lympus all over the Greek Empire." T-266 boasted. "We will order the human primitives to do as we command."

"But you've only got one bull-god,"
McMoo pointed out. "Isn't it going to
take Farmer Moos quite a while to tour
round an empire?"

"Farmer Moos is our leader. But now
other F.B.I. agents will step forward to
rule the human city-states on his behalf."
T-266 turned round and gestured:
"Behold the Moo-lympians – deities of
doom!"

McMoo and Yak swapped nervous
looks as menacing figures strode along
the tunnel towards them.

A blonde-haired ter-moo-nette – a
female ter-moo-nator with yellow eyes,
six-inch steel stiletto heels and a chrome
udder – was first to approach.

"Meet the wife of Farmer Moos," said
T-266.

McMoo snorted. "The wife of Zeus
was called Hera, wasn't she?"

"I am *Hay*-ra," the ter-moo-nette
informed him, then gestured to a

gigantic, shaggy bull in a spiky helmet. "And this is the Greek god of war – Hairies."

"*Ares*," McMoo replied. "Hairies indeed!"

"Sorry to keep you waiting," said Hairies in a surprisingly high voice, "but we simply *had* to finish our fabulous new costumes so we could show them off before squishing you."

Hay-ra frowned. "And because we were discussing evil plans, right?"

"Oh, yes." Hairies giggled. "And evil plans too, of course."

Another ter-moo-nette stepped forward. This one had dark hair, horns

entwined with vines, and a crossbow mounted on her udder. "I am the Greek goddess of hunting," she said.

McMoo pondered. "That was Artemis, wasn't it?"

"Yes, but men shall call me Arty-*moos*."

Still more F.B.I. "gods" emerged in ever more flamboyant costumes, outnumbering the C.I.A. agents six to one.

"We shall command that they hold the Moo-lympic Games every four *weeks* instead of every four years," said Hay-ra, "and open them to *all* people."

Hairies nodded. "The Romans. The Egyptians. The Persians. The Celts . . ."

"An audience of millions," Arty-moos agreed.

Yak gasped. "And while the different human tribes and their leaders enjoy their sport, the brain-beetles will be going to work on them too – so *they* will come to worship cattle as well."

Hay-ra nodded. "They will live for us and die for us. The human world will become evil cow heaven!"

McMoo stamped an angry hoof. "The F.B.I. has come up with some rotten plans in its time, but this one takes the biscuit!" He paused. "Actually, I could just eat a biscuit right now. With a nice cup of tea. Any chance of tea?"

"No," said Hay-ra. "We have enjoyed our little gloat—"

"And our fashion show!" squealed Hairies.

"But now," said Arty-moos, "it is high time that you and your friends were ter-moo-nated."

McMoo backed away across the courtyard as the evil F.B.I. cattle-gods started to close in . . .

Chapter Eleven

A FIGHTING CHANCE

"Ready for the fight of your life, Yak?" said McMoo grimly.

"Always." Yak jumped up – and oddly, T-122 didn't try to stop him. "But if we're going to take on these creeps, Professor, we'll need back-up."

McMoo frowned. "But Bo's flat out in the shed – isn't she?"

"Nope." Yak suddenly yanked off T-122's dented helmet – to reveal the face of Little Bo! "Check it out."

Bo beamed at the boggling McMoo. "Yak was fibbing before, Prof! We *did* beat dumb old T-122. Then I pulled off his armour . . ."

"And put on a *real* fashion show to fool these F.B.I. drongos." Yak winked at her. "We wanted to lure the 'Moo-lympians' out of hiding so we could get them all at once."

"It is still twelve against three," hissed Hay-ra.

"That's what you think," Bo retorted. "We've got reinforcements, ready to come out as soon as they hear the signal."

McMoo's eyebrows shot up. "The C.I.A.?"

"More like the B.I.A.," said Yak. "Bandits In Action!" Turning to the Time Shed, he gave a loud whistle. "All right, Andros – time for you and your boys to earn that treasure I told you about . . ."

To the professor's amazement, the

bandits he and Yak had battled in
the hills came pouring out of the
shed! Yelling and roaring, they hurled
themselves at the dressed-up bulls.

"Where did they come from?" McMoo
marvelled as Andros decked Hairies with
a punch to the snout.

"When you and I first landed and
went out to find Pat and Bo, we must've
left the shed's doors open," said Yak,

dodging an arrow fired from Arty-moos's deadly udder. "The bandits hid there when they ran from Pericles's guards. They were still hiding behind the hay bales when T-122 brought us back here."

Bo nodded, blasting Hay-ra with cold milk from her udder. "I saw Yak leaning over a hay bale and thought he was being sick. But he was actually talking Andros into helping us."

Andros clobbered a bull-god and flashed his gap-toothed smile. "With the riches we raid from here, I can give up banditry and open a nice souvenir stand at the Olympic track."

"First we have to make sure the Olympics don't remain *Moo*-lympics for ever," cried McMoo, hurling an old cowpat in Arty-moos's face.

The ter-moo-nette tried to shoot him with a cream-cheese cannon, but hit Hairies instead.

"You've ruined my costume!" The bull-god of war burst into tears and was quickly brought down by a group of bandits.

"We're winning!" Bo cried, swinging Hay-ra into another of the bogus bull-gods.

"And while Bo was dressing up as T-122 – ready to pretend I was her prisoner – I found that the shed had just enough power to send a message to the C.I.A.," Yak revealed. "They should be here any time now."

McMoo was about to heave a sigh of relief when he heard the familiar roar of jets kicking in. He looked around in sudden panic. "The jet-ship – it's taking off. Someone's getting away!"

Bo looked around and scowled. "There's no sign of T-266. It must be him."

"And I bet he'll be heading for Mount Moo-lympus," the professor shouted over the din. "If he fires the 'switch-off' ray, it will deactivate the beetles and leave Pat and forty thousand Greeks believing Farmer Moos is their lord and master. The F.B.I. can still win!"

The jet-ship rose up through a haze of smoke behind the courtyard wall. McMoo saw T-266 at the controls, sticking out his mechanical tongue.

"Quick, Bo – the Time Shed!" McMoo pointed to the tatty building. "The tow-ropes are still attached. Perhaps we can tag along."

"Do it!" Yak snapped, helping Andros to trip another F.B.I. agent. "We'll take care of things here."

There was no time to argue. The Time Shed was already starting to leave the ground.

"What's happening?" A weak and wobbly T-122 staggered into sight in the shed doorway, wearing nothing but a pair of spotty underpants.

"'Scuse me," said Bo, using the ter-moo-nator as a stepladder to help her climb up onto the roof. As she did so, T-122 overbalanced and crashed to the courtyard floor.

"'Scuse me too!" McMoo used the robo-bull's techno-tum as a springboard

to launch himself
through the air, just
managing to grab
onto the shed in the
nick in time. A moment
later, T-266 gunned the
jet-ship's engines and sped
away – with two unexpected
passengers along for the ride . . .

Back in Olympia, Pat felt like a
sleepwalker as he followed Farmer Moos
and the crowd of leaders and spectators
over to Mount Moo-lympus.

The Games had gone on all afternoon.
After beating the Greeks at the pole
vault, the oxen had gone on to thrash
them at the javelin and the discus. With
each trouncing, Pat had seen the humans

129

growing more and more certain that cows were superior creatures and that Farmer Moos was their true ruler. Pat longed to show them they were wrong; that they needed to fight back against Moos. But he felt as though he was trapped in a dismal daydream and he couldn't snap out of it.

"Follow me, everyone," Farmer Moos commanded. "No dawdling."

"You heard Great Farmer Moos!" shouted Pericles. "Show him proper respect. Quick march!"

"But you are all-powerful, Farmer Moos," Pat said sleepily. "Why the sudden rush?"

"There has been an incident back at base," Moos replied crossly. "I must finalize the thoughts of these human fools – and yours – without delay."

Soon the strange, silent procession came to the first crusty slopes of the imposing muck-mountain.

"Behold the glory of Mount Moo-lympus!" cried Diagoras.

Farmer Moos checked his watch. "T-266 will arrive in the jet-ship within minutes . . ."

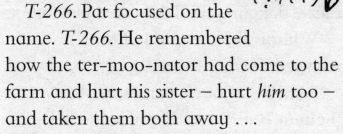

T-266. Pat focused on the name. *T-266.* He remembered how the ter-moo-nator had come to the farm and hurt his sister – hurt *him* too – and taken them both away . . .

The more he thought about it, the angrier he became. And the angrier he became, the clearer he began to think. *T-266 is my enemy. The F.B.I. is my enemy.* "Farmer Moos is my enemy!" blurted Pat.

Moos glared at him. "What's that, boy?"

"I said, you're my enemy." Pat pushed out his chin. "I've beaten your brainwashing."

"Then you are of no further use to me," Moos told him. He raised his electric hoof, ready to fire . . .

Then the swoosh of firing jets filled the sky. Pat looked up; and, like the crowds around him, he gave the biggest gasp of his life as the F.B.I. jet-ship came into sight – dangling the Time Shed beneath it.

"What is the meaning of this?" bellowed Farmer Moos.

"Is this not your glorious work, O Great Bull?" asked Pericles. "There are cows up there."

Pat nodded dumbly. There certainly *were* cows up there! Balanced on the shed roof as though riding a giant surfboard, Professor McMoo cheered on Little Bo, who was climbing the tow-rope up to the underside of the ship.

"You must get inside, Bo!" McMoo shouted. "Quickly!"

Up in the air, Bo quickly climbed to the

top of the tow rope
and started scaling the
side of the ship.
Desperately, she battered
on the passenger door
with all her strength.
Finally the hinges
buckled and with a
last, mighty tug she
ripped the door off
completely.

T-266 almost jumped
out of the driver's seat at the sight of
Bo hanging there in the doorway. Then
he struck out with a hefty bronze hoof
to push her to her doom. But instead
of dodging the blow, Bo grabbed hold
of the ter-moo-nator's arm and tugged

with all her strength. Warbling with surprise, T-266 was jerked sideways out of his seat, lost his balance and tumbled past her – falling from the ship and crash-landing in the giant dung heap . . .

"Nooooooo!" cried Farmer Moos. "The humans mustn't be distracted now. It could ruin their brainwashing."

"I thought as much," McMoo hollered, still perched on the shed roof. The jet-ship swung this way and that above Mount Moo-lympus as Little Bo climbed into the pilot's seat. "Bo, you'd better learn to drive this thing quickly – before my breakfast makes a surprise reappearance."

"Stop distracting my brainwashed humans, Professor" – Farmer Moos pointed his deadly hoof at Pat – "or your young friend dies!"

Chapter Twelve

MOO-LYMPIC GOLD

Pat froze in fear. He tried to judge whether he could jump and overpower the F.B.I. agent before the hoof went off . . .

But Bo had wasted no time working out which button fired the jet-ship's laser beams. *ZZAP!* The grass between Pat and Moos exploded in flames. Pericles and the other leaders gasped, and the crowd of spectators shrank back in horror.

"Oxen," Moos commanded, "you must get Pat Vine – the milk cow can't zap you all."

Pat backed away up the sticky slopes of Mount Moo-lympus as the lean bull-athletes spread out to get him. But Farmer

Moos had underestimated Bo's skills as she fired lasers at the oxen again and again. Finally their nerve broke and they scattered in all directions.

"Sweet!" yelled Bo. "The trainer trashes her pupils."

"STOP!" Farmer Moos looked anxiously at the terrified crowd. "I said *no distractions*. I can't lose control of these ancient Greek goons now!"

"Perhaps you'd better just zap me?" McMoo took careful hold of the tow-rope. "You know, take care of me once and for all."

"An excellent idea," the mad bull roared, taking careful aim with his electric hoof. "Goodbye, McMoo!"

To Pat's horror, Farmer Moos unleashed a blue bolt of electrical power. But at the last moment McMoo scooted up the tow-rope, and the energy blast sliced the steel strand neatly in two just below his hooves. "Good shot!" cheered

the professor – as, to Pat's shock, the
Time Shed plummeted from the sky.

KA-*SQUELCH!*

The shed smashed down on top of
Mount Moo-lympus. Spectacular purple
sparks zigzagged down the dung heap,
quickly followed by a blinding flash of

blue light. Unable to take any more, the terrified spectators turned and bolted, pounding back towards the Olympic fields. Only Pericles and his fellow leaders remained, still transfixed by the incredible show.

McMoo, still holding tight to what remained of the tow-rope, beamed down at his enemies. "Whoops! Looks like that crash-landing fused the shed's energy banks. Thought that might happen – what a distraction, eh? Seems to have broken through your brainwashing."

"Quickly, Bo!" Pat bellowed. "Switch off the beetles before Moos can get them working again!"

A few moments later, a ruby-red ray shone out from the jet-ship, irradiating the area.

"Gah!" Farmer Moos start to blub. "You'll be sorry for this, McMoo."

"I'm sorry already," the professor admitted. "Repairing the Time Shed's going to take me ages!"

Moos raised his hoof to fire at the professor again, but Bo blasted him with lasers. He jumped with fright and fell into an especially nasty soft patch of cow dung. "Mission abort," he wailed, pulling a large silver disk from under his robes – an F.B.I. time machine. "Mission abort!"

And in the blink of an eye and a whiff of black smoke, the F.B.I. baddie was gone.

"Yayyy!" cheered Pat. He was bashed and bruised and dirty and puffed out, but had never felt happier in his life.

Bo took the jet-ship down, and once McMoo had jumped from the tow-rope to safety, she parked it clumsily behind the smoking Time Shed. Pat ran up the mucky rise to give the two of them a massive hug.

"Tidy work, boys," said Bo. "We won!"

"But what about Pericles and all the other leaders?" asked Pat, frowning.

"All these crazy things they've seen . . . the way the Olympics were messed up . . . surely that might change history?"

McMoo frowned. "I hope not." He pulled out his ringblender, so humans couldn't understand him. Then he trotted over to Pericles and Diagoras, who were standing at the bottom of the quietly steaming slope.

"What happened?" Pericles scratched his head. "How did we get here?"

Diagoras shrugged. "My mind's a blank."

"They've forgotten everything!" said McMoo with relief. "Now the brainwashing's worn off, the memories have faded too. It'll be the same for everyone, I bet. A few of them, like the athletes, might be sore for a while — but they'll put that down to too much partying the night before and start the Olympics all over again."

"Come, Diagoras," said Pericles firmly. "We are great leaders – and great leaders do not waste time hanging around dung heaps. We're here to enjoy the Olympics, and by great Zeus, that's what we will do!"

Bo smiled as the men walked away. "They believe in Zeus again, not Moos," she noted. "Still dumb – but a lot better!"

"And I'm a lot better for seeing you're all safe," called a familiar gruff voice.

"Yakky-kins!" Bo squealed with

delight to find that the big black bull had emerged from a newly arrived C.I.A. time machine shaped like an enormous milk crate. Several cows in purple sashes came coolly out behind him. "Oh, and here's our back-up – finally!"

"Sorry we're late," said Yak. "It took a while to lock up the Moo-lympians and clear the future technology from their secret base. We've let the bandits take what's left – now that they've promised to go straight."

The professor nodded approvingly. "I hope Andros's Olympic souvenir stall is a great success."

"Farmer Moos got away, worst luck," sighed Bo. "But those oxen of his are still about."

"We'll catch them and put them in jail," Yak vowed. "And we'll also gather up all the dung and the brain-beetles, just in case."

Pat was puzzled. "How will you do that?"

"Those insects live in dung, right? Well, we've got the best dung-shoveller around."

Yak hauled a snoring Barmo out of the
C.I.A. time machine.

Pat chuckled. "Looks like it's all been
too much for her!"

"Let her rest while she can," said Yak.
"When she wakes up she's got to shift
that mega-muck pile!"

"And so Mount Moo-lympus will
crumble," McMoo observed. "Just like

the F.B.I.'s dreams of conquest."

Yak nodded. "The F.B.I. are never completely beaten, but we scored a big victory today, troops. Now I'd better scoot and tidy up the loose ends. My technical team will help you fix the Time Shed – then you can go home."

"I can't wait," said Pat. "To think we complained of being bored!"

Bo nodded. "A bit of peace and quiet sounds good to me."

"Then you'd better hope Bessie Barmer stays knocked out for a while," said McMoo with a grin. "We'll race home, have a cuppa, and look forward to our next mission. Because when it comes to fighting time-crime, our little team wins *Moo*-lympic gold every time!"

Meet the time-travelling cows
for the first time!

THE TER-MOO-NATORS
by Steve Cole

IT'S 'UDDER' MADNESS!

Genius cow Professor
McMoo and his trusty
sidekicks, Pat and Bo,
are the star agents of
the C.I.A. – short for
COWS IN ACTION!
They travel through
time, fighting evil bulls
from the future and
keeping history on
the right track . . .

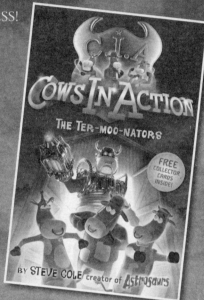

When Professor
McMoo invents a brilliant
TIME MACHINE, he and his friends are soon
attacked by a terrifying TER-MOO-NATOR – a
deadly robo-cow who wants to mess with the past
and change the future! And that's only the start of an
incredible ADVENTURE that takes McMoo, Pat and
Bo from a cow paradise in the future to the SCARY
dungeons of King Henry VIII . . .

It's time for action. COWS IN ACTION!

ISBN: 978 1 862 30189 4

Riddle of the Raptors

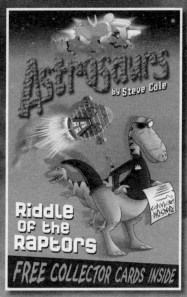

Astrosaurs
*Riddle of
the Raptors*
By Steve Cole

BLAST OFF!

Teggs is no ordinary dinosaur – he's an **Astrosaur**!
Captain of the amazing spaceship DSS *Sauropod*, he goes on
dangerous missions and fights evil – along with his faithful
crew, Gypsy, Arx and Iggy!

When a greedy gang of meat-eating raptors raid the
Sauropod and kidnap two top athletes, Teggs and his crew
race to the rescue. But there's more to the raptors' plot than
meets the eye. Can Teggs solve their rascally riddle in time?

Collect your very own Astrosaurs cards! Included in the back
of each book.

ISBN: 978 0 099 47294 0

Visit www.**stevecolebooks**.co.uk for fun, games, jokes, to meet the characters and much, much more!

Welcome to a world where dinosaurs fly spaceships and cows use a time-machine . . .

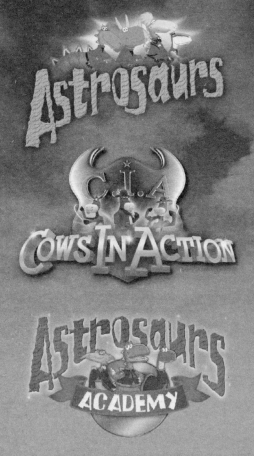

Sign up for the Steve Cole monthly newsletter to find out what your favourite author is up to!